Khawaish Likhne Ki

Flairs and Glairs
Publication House

"Khawaish Likhne Ki

ISBN No: " 9789391302993"
1st Edition
Language – English and Hindi

Flairs and Glairs
Publication House
Regd. Under MSME Act.

Disclaimer

This is a work of fiction and solely represent the thoughts of the corresponding authors of the articles. Our editors have tried their best to edit the content of all the authors and check the plagiarism.

All the write-ups in this book are unique and are only published in this book.

In case any plagiarism or error is found, only the author is responsible alone, and not the publisher or the Compilers.

Cover Designing and Book Formatting
Shubham Shah and Ishani Agarwal

Co Author

Shubham Shah (Founder Flairs and Glairs)
Ishani Agarwal (Co-Founder Flairs and Glairs)
1. Divyadharshini R
2. Gayatri Tirmare
3. RK Nathan
4. Kajal Pandey
5. Ujjaini Chatterjee
6. Raktim Kashyap
7. Omkesh Rodge
8. Kirti Goel
9. Dr Rakesh R Mund
10. Miss Shruti Prakash
11. Pujitha Mallareddi
12. Bibiayeesha Mulla
13. Ujjwal Sharan
14. Dipshikha Mohanty
15. Sneha Dubey
16. Rajesh Satpate
17. Nuzair Fathima
18. Shivi Goyal
19. Prachi Sharma
20. Yashvi Yashi Srivastava
21. Ayushi Sharma
22. Nilesh Vispute

Shubham Shah

(Founder- Flairs and Glairs)

Shubham Shah, an entrepreneur at "Flairs & Glairs" a brand with dynamics in events organizing and cultural educational pan INDIA, is a 26yrs old guy who recently has entered the digital platform of imprinting emotions. He has initiated with his own open mic platform to help budding poets and aspiring writers under his brand named as "Teekhe Zasbaaat"

He is a commerce graduate from the Bhagalpur City of Bihar. He states Writing has impersonated him since childhood and he has now been writing for over a decade!

Cooking, on the other hand, is his passion! He also mentions, trying out new things just tickles him!

When asked sir, Why SPICY EMOTIONS?

He smiled and added, "agar jasbaat teekhe na ho toh wo jasbaat kahan" Spices are all that blends! So do his words!

As a chef, he presents to you his dish! Hot and freshly served! Taste it! Feel it! Enjoy it! You can also find his writing in the Book "Teekhe Zasbaaat" and 50+ Co -authored anthologies. With his passion to explore opportunities across Platforms, he is working with keen dev otion and We wish him all the very best for his future ventures.

He is Featured in the International Magazine DeMode for his upcoming solo novel.

He is Approved by Ne8x for its Lit Fest, and is a Golden Star Awards 2020 Winner.

He is a India Book of Records Holder for his Anthology Satrang, and has the Grandmaster title by Asia Book of Records, for the same.

He has also been featured in Prabhat Khabar, Dainik Jagran, and a lot of other Newspapers in Bihar for his achievements.

He has been a proud co-author to

India Book Of Records (Title- Black)

World Book Of Records (Title -15 Wonders of Poetries)

India Book Of Records (Title - Aaina)

Vajra World Records Holder (Title - Gustakhi Maaf Hai)

High Range of Records Holder (Title - Gustakhi Maaf Hai)

Indian Book of Records

(Title - Road from Worst to Best)

Share your reviews on his

INSTAGRAM

@spicy_emotions
@shubham4shah

Or via email on

shubham2shah@gmail.com

To stay tuned to his work and opportunities follow his business Handles

INSTAGRAM   FACEBOOK   YOUTUBE

@flairsandglairs
@teekhezasbaaat

WEBSITE:

https://flairsandglairs.in/
https://flairsandglairs.com/

Ishani Agarwal

(Co-Founder- Flairs and Glairs)

Ishani Agarwal hails from the City of Joy, Kolkata.
She is the co -founder of her Community "Teekhe Zasbaaat" and Flairs and Glairs Publication.
Been a Compiler for 45+ Anthologies, she is in the process for more. Co-authored in 150+ Anthologies. She is a India Book of Records Holder, a Vajra World Records Holder, a High Range of Records Holder, an OMG Book of Records Holder, a Bravo Record holder, a Forever Star Book of World Records and an Indian Book of Records Holder.
Approved by Ne8x for its Lit Fest 2020, and Literary Icon 2020. Also a Golden Star Awards Winner 2020.
She has also been award ed with India Star Republic Award 2021, a part of She Awards by Awards Arc and Winner of Nari Samman 2021 by Literoma.

She is also selected as Best Achiever of the Year by AwardsArc and Most Challenging Compiler Award by Spectrum Awards.
She got her first solo Published,a solo Compilation consisting of first 750 contents of hers, titled "Hand That Burnt While Healing".

She has been featured by the National Magazine "Taree Zameen Par" with the title 'unstoppable'.
Also featured in the International Magazine DeMode for her upcoming solo novel, she is proud to write on social issues, and is happy with the love she is receiving.
Connect with her on Instagram: @Ishani_agarwal_quotes / @compilations_so_far

Divyadharshini R

Divyadharshini R, an MA English and Bachelor of Education graduate. Born on 15th May, 1995 in Honnatty, Kotagiri, The Nilgiris. As a student in the past, planned to achieve more, yet possessed with obstacles. An upcoming poet with intention of becoming successful one day.

An Island Dream

Wide opened eye lids
Surrounded with greenery
Walked through wet leaves
Ways to somewhere.

Touched the droplets of tip
Fingers shivered and attracted veins
Roamed around what's next
Stood in a cliff and saw.

Flows like a storm never believed
Splashes through rock and sparkles
Sunlight shone bright
Water twinkles like mirror.

Beat up with a water
Body shrills and happiness bounds
Played like a kid never been
Physique got wet as well mental.

Turning around found none
Sported through lane
Found a big border sand
Thereby an ocean.

Running over water and fell
Feets were swinging with foam
Rummaging someone would alive
None present never mind.

Someone knocked the door
Searching for it but nothing
Knock! Knock! Knock!
It's time to wake from dream.

Gayatri Tirmare

Dream big and achieve it is the agenda of my life. I started my writing from the age of 15. Basically, I am forensic science student (2nd yr.) And passionate about writing because I believe that this is the better way to express our emotions or thought.

<u>गाथा एक वीर जवान की।</u>

मुझे आज भी याद है वोह दिन जब उसका जन्मदिन था,उसके बालों में गजरा लगते वक्त उस गजरे की महकती खुशबू में वही छोड़ आया था।जिसने उसकी सारी खुशी छोड़ कर मुझे अपना फ़र्ज़ निभाने को कहा था वोह जान थी मेरी जिसने मुझे हौसला दिलाया था।

ये लोग क्यों नहीं समजते हैं होती तो एक ही रिवाज एक ही रसम हैं, बस कुछ अंदाज बदल जाते हैं।वरना एक ही बात है जिसे कुछ उपवास तो कोई रमज़ान कहते हैं।

मुझे आज भी याद है वोह दिन जिस दिन मेरे घर में एक नन्ही सी चिड़िया अयी थी , उसकी मीठी सी मुस्कान ने मुझे हौसला दिलाया था वोह बेटी थी मेरी जिसे में वैसेही चहकता छोड़ आया था।

ये लोक क्यों नहीं जानते, की कोई पूजे पत्थर को तो कोई सजदे में अपने सर झुकाते हैं ।वरना ये एक ही बात है जनाब कोई इसे पूजा तो कोई इसे अपना ईमान बनाते हैं।

तुझसे भारत माता बस एक गुजारिश हैं मेरी अब की तेरी सीने से मुझे लगाये रखना क्युकी वोह मां थी मेरी जिसके बहो को में यूहीं तरसता छोड़ आया था।

आखिर ये भेद भाव कब जाकर खत्म होगा, अब तो मरना जीना बस इस तिरंगे के नाम होगा और अग्ला जन्म लिया तो मेरा देश हिंदुस्तान ही होगा

RK Nathan

Channelize The Affection.

Everyone wants to be together and forever.
Is it possible to be.
Obviously yes.
How to maintain sustain and retain the relationship forever by being together.
The prime key to retain the relationship in a healthy parameter is to have a better clarity of our own limitations and boundaries with the relation concerned.
The second key is to respect their emotions and their time as well.
Everyone must act under one sun and one moon.
It is an emotional contact/contract and mental connect of the spirit through the physical medium.
Sometimes we feel the connect and the presence of the beloved who left us or who passed away.
It is purely about spirit and soul.
Less expectation between can harmonize the caring, channelize the affection, tunes the bond.
One must possess the smartness to embrace the beloved one though there is a difference of opinion even there is a contrast in the ideas.
Mutual understanding incarcerates the intimacy tightly together and forever.
Being selflessness breaks the ego and builds the frame of mind.
Selflessness is not a sacrifice. It is just taking care with little more concern.
True love brings r eal satisfaction into the heart when it starts supply love for the beloved.
The mechanism of the heart is designed to devote. Devote with determination.

Kajal Pandey

Kajal Pandey
Branch manager of Aditya birla sunlife Pvt. LTD
One who loves to write for self-peace and of course for getting
the recognition.

Maa Baap Hamara Jahaan Hote Hai

Maa baap hamara jahaan hote Hai ,
Bina jameen ki is duniya me hamara aasmaan hote Hai.
Mana bat bat par yeh humse naraaj hote Hai, Par door kahin
hume hui hamari thodi si takleef se bhi ye kitna pareshaan
hote Hai...
Bina jameen ki is jindagi me maa baap hi hamara asmaan hote
hai.

Badalte Jazbaat

Voh Jo mohabbat kehte the Hame aaj mohabbat karne se
katraate hai.
Door Gaya ho jab koi dil se fir vo Kahan hi kabhi laut Kar aa
pate hai .
Rokne ki koshish us waqt ko to   ham har baar karte hai, Par
afsos khud ko khud ke   haathon ham majboor aksar hi patee
hai Aur voh hai ki keh Kar bhi Kahan mohabbat nibha paate
hai .
Anchahe hi har pal
ham waqt ko hathon se chhotta sa mehsoos Kar paate hai, Par
fir bhi ham Kahan hi khud ko kabhi khud rok paate hai

Aakhir kaise badalte waqt ke saath jazbaat badal jaate hai?

Kashmkash Hai Jindagi

Kyo hum aksar dimaag ki to har khwaaish poori Kar dete hai,
Itna sab Kar ke bhi raat me use chain see sone ka haq bhi de
dete hai...
Par dil ka Kya? kyo Jo chaaha vo na paa sake Jo bhaaya man
ko laakh koshishon ke baad bhi na use apna bna sake....
Tees si ho jaati hai jab anjaane hi kahin vo dil   ki chahatein
yaad aati hai.
Dil aur dimaag ki ladaai me ham sada hi dimaag ko chhor dil
aur uski chahaton ko dabate hai,

Waqt beetta jataa hai usi beette waqt ke saath un chahaton
ke saath anjaane hi hum   hmara sukoon bhi dafn Kar jaate
jai ....

Kyo hum aksar dil aur dimaag ke beech dimaag ko chunte hai
aur use hi sunte hai

Ujjaini Chatterjee

Kathak dancer. Vegan. Bohemian soul. Loves to be with nature.

Ek Khat

"Hum hamesha saath rahenge". Kitne ajeeb hai na yeh lafz. Matlab hum yeh lafz ek doosre ko bolte toh hain lekin, phir alabatta usse nibhana bhul jate hain. Aur phir humare paas reh jati hain yeh bachpane mein kiye huye vado ke yaadein, jo hamesha humare saath reh jati hain. Ajeeb hain na, rishte toot jate hain, zindagiyaan badal jati hain, kitne meelon ke fasle ajaate hain do jismon ke darmiyaan. Lekin yeh dil hain ki har jaga un bematalab yaadon ko apne saath liye chalta hain. Dekho aaj hum dono main kitni duriyaa hain lekin, hamaari roohe jaise ek doosre ke naam ki gaath bandhe huye hain. Puraane dino ko yaad karti hu toh hasi aati hain lekin kuch dard bhi mehsoos hota hain. Hasi yeh yaad karke aati hain ke, jab bhi hum alag se akele kahi milne ka teh karte the toh kuch na kuch garbar hoti hi thi, kabhi tum busy toh kabhi hum quad. Aur dard yeh yaad karke ata hain ke jab humare ghar valo ko humare bade mein pata chala toh na jaane baba se kitni maar khaaye aur maa se kitne taane sune. Phir bhi mera dil tha   ke tumhe pyaar karne se baaz nahi ata tha. Khair iss zindagi mein na sahi toh agli zindagi mein hamaari mohabbat kaabil zarur hogi, bas humaari yaadein hamesha saath rakhna. Khuda Hafiz.

Raktim Kashyap

A boy from Guwahati, Assam, currently perusing LL. B and love to write or can be said as love to play with pen, already written in many anthologies and can write in nearly more than 2 language including national and regional

"The Night to Admire"

The wind blows
The night acquires
Still, I am here,
Waiting for
The glimpse of snow
Shining in the mountain higher.
The sound makes an Ecco
And Whispering the feelings of love,
In front of the bonfire
Holding the hands
Being high above.

"You and Me"

When the whole world sits
In the fire of faithlessness
I find
The rain of your love,
To forget all my enxitis
The cute little lips of your's
Are enough.
When I saw into your eyes
I forgot myself,
I just get deep and deep down
When the night
Tik the clock at twelve.

"My Loved Destiny"

Do you feel
What I do,
By looking at the sky of blue.
I can never forget
The first day I meet you,
You became my destiny.

Omkesh Rodge

I am Omkesh Rodge from Udgir . I am pursing B.tech degree in mechanical engineering.I am beginner in writer's world and hope to rise up here.Writing is my hobby. Recently started writing for anthologies

A Lovely Hug

That day they had a fight. It was not usual for them to fight this long. Situation went blue for me. They raised their volume to their highest. I was scared. The scenario was so scary that I thought horror films were less scary. My heart rate was high. I was so young to understandtheir reasons but I still kept listening to them form the next room.
Mom said this and that, dad said this and that. They blamed each other. As time was passing, the fight was getting worse. I started crying because they didn't stop. My head was going numb. All my senses got dull. I wasthirsty but could not drink water. I was hungry but could not eat . I sat leaning against the wall. They did not hit each other but that whole scene was already more than worse for me. All I could do was just sit crying. I haven't did anything wrong   but s till did not have enough courage to face them. I was afraid of them
now. They did not notice that I was home from playground.

Clock moved its hand three hrs. more. Mom finally came out of the room. She was angry. Her full red face and stamping of feet would tell that. She went to bathroom and washed her face. Before she would notice I wiped my tears washed my face in basin. I just gave happy smile and looked at her as if I did not know anything. She kept looking at
me for bit. Her face felt so satisfactory as if I met her after a long time.
Then came dad. Even he had the same expression. They look at me and then gazed at each other. They both came near me. The environment went silent suddenly for me. I was in the center.
Both off them hugged me as if it was our last day together. I was surprised and my head went blank. All I could feel was the warmth and love of their hug.

I started breathing heavily. Suddenly tears came down   from my eyes. I could not control them. My n ose started flowing. None of my body part was obeying my brains order.   Within few seconds I wet their shoulders with my tears. They suddenly looked at me and now I could see fear in their eyes. "What happened dear?" she asked. I could not speak anything. They understood that I have heard them fighting. "You don't need to cry. We were fighting with a devil in   there that was here to take you." Dad lied in energetic voice. I stopped crying with breaking breaths and played along with
him and smiled again. In a gentle "I love you mom and dad. Don't let me go." Mom and dad looked at me and gave a smile. Their eyes were wet too but tears did not roll down. My hands could not cover a single one but I tried to give them both a tight hug.

Kirti Goel

The writer of this poem is Kirti Goel. Vivacious and lively by nature. She believes in living her life to fullest. The writer had started writing poetry as her hobby and her interest in writing has developed over time when her work started getting appreciated. She has written some very well drafted poetry which can be reached at her Instagram page @poetryy_fair This poetry she believes can touch the hearts of her readers especially who are in long distance relationship!!

Long Distance Relationship!!

People say love didn't last
When you are apart...
But, I feel you in my breath everyday....

I feel you in my Ink
When I write for you
I see you in my dreams
When I think about you..

I feel your 'presence'
When I miss you everyday..
I feel your warmth
When I cuddle the pillow everyday.....

They say....
Love didn't last when you are apart
I say....
My love Will last..
till my last !!!!

Dr Rakesh R Mund

Dr Rakesh R Mund has been participating in more than 15 anthologies. His educational background in MBBS has given broad base which to approach medical and scientific topics. He fund to read veda and diffrent literatures which give a glimpse on his writing.
You can contact with him: insta- Rakeshmundr_

दूर होके भी पास

नहीं मालूम करती तु
क्या वहाँ पे,
नहीं मालूम रहती तु
काहाँ काहाँ पे,
लेकिन जब मेरा दिल
धडकता है,
तब तब बस तेरा नाम
याद आता है ।

हाँ शायद इसलिए नाम
इसका प्रेम है,
दूर रहकर संपर्क अतुट
जीसका प्रेम है ,
बस ऐक भरोसा ऐसा की
संबंध कायम है,
पास रहकर प्यार जताना
थोड़ी ना नियम है ।

जब जब रात को गगन
को देखता हूँ,
शायद वो चाँद होगा जीसे
मैं तु समझता हूँ,
क्या भी करुं इश्क़ है ही
ऐसा मेरा तूझसे,
ह्वाट्सएप भी लगता है
पार्क अब मुझसे ।

चल झुठ मत वोल प्रिये

क्या तु है उदास ?
आरे हम तो खुश हैं दूर रहके
नहीं है बकबास,
वो नजदीक रहने वाले भला
क्या जानें ,
जब कुछ समय बाद मिलना
सच होता सपनें ।

फिर क्यों डरना जब दो दिल
धडके ऐक नाम,
दूर होके भी पास ओर हासिल
होगा हमारे मुकाम,
फर्क सिर्फ इतना वो बाहोँ में
लेके प्यार करते,
हम ख्वाबों मैं रोज़ नये नये
रेस्टोरेंट घुमते ।

Miss Shruti Prakash

My self-Miss Shruti Prakash. I am from Rarebareli, Uttar Pradesh. I am 22 years old working as a Clinical instructor in Nursing College. I am dedicated towards my inking because I believe, this is God gift to me so it should not be hide   that's why I love to write.

(1)

We have not met for years longest,
But we know each other the best!
We have so many difficulties,
But we take each other's responsibilities!
We might be in deep pain oceans,
But we will never show our real emotions!
I deal with the world like war,
He is My strength doesn't matter if he is far!
We live in the world of sacrifice and hope,
It gives us the strength to cope!
My silence he heard a loud,
He always gets to know when I am under the stress Cloud!
I meet a lot of people in the world,
But I am in love with his eternal word!
We both drive in the sea of love, this battleship;
We are the Couple in Long distance relationship!

(2)

हर आशिक इश्क पर कुर्बान नहीं होता,
शब-ओ-रोज़ मिले महबूब इस गर्दिश में,
खुदा आशिकों पर इतना मेहरबान नहीं होता,
ये कहर, उलझन, बेताबी तो लाजमी है प्रकाश,
ये दूरियों का इश्क इतना आसान नहीं होता,
यू दर्द में मुस्कुराना उस हंसी के लिए,
यू अश्क़ को छुपाना उस सुलह के लिए,
बेशर्त मोहब्बत का यहाँ कोई मुकाम नहीं होता,
ये दूरियों का इश्क इतना आसान नहीं होता,
उसकी छवि खुद के अक्ष में निहारना,
उसकी हर फरमाइश को मुसलसल मानना,
अपनी जान पर सब कुछ वरना,
कोई एहसान नहीं होता,
बेशर्त मोहब्बत का यहाँ कोई मुकाम नहीं होता,
दिल में दर्द पर चेहरे पर कोई निशान नहीं होता,
ये दूरियों का इश्क इतना आसान नहीं होता ।

Pujitha Mallareddi

This is Pujitha Mallareddi a student doctor of pharmacy in viswanadha institute of pharmaceutical sciences from Visakhapatnam. She strongly believes   writings are not just phrases, they are emotions that last even after our phase.

Eternal Love

My love, I don't exactly remember the day we met, but it was the luckiest day of my life.
I still remember the way we talked, the way we smiled, the way we stalked, the way we cared.
I still can't forget the way you blushed in my presence and even at a whisper of my name.
I remember the way our eyes spoke in mime, compiling lots of stories.
Your fragrance is still on my   heart sometimes making me weep and sometimes blush.
Though you are too far for my hands to hold you,
But your image in my heart will cherish until my last breath.

My Soul

Our bond is like an ocean,
With emotions as its depth,
Care as its width,
Anger as its storm,
Tears as sprinkling rain.
Our distance is just a barrier,
It can never be a reason because you are not just my love, you are my soul,
 and my love for you never ends until the largest oceans dry and never ends until I die.

Forever and Always

Life may turn into topsy-turvy,
Things may be tossed on to other side,
But my love for you never changes,
As the bright sun in the morning,
And as twinkling stars at night.

Bibiayeesha Mulla

Bibiayeesha
From Karnataka
Dentistry is my profession
Poetry is my passion

(1)

जब मोहब्बत हो गहरी तो फासलों से फ़र्क़ नहीं पड़ता
जब मेहबूब हो बेमिसाल तो दुनिया से फ़र्क़ नहीं पड़ता

तुम मुझसे दूर ज़रूर हो पर मेरे दिल के क़रीब हो
फासले जितने भी आये दिल की धड़कन तुम हो

(2)

मोहब्बत तो बेपनाह थी उस शख्स से पर
फसलों ने दूरियां बड़ा दी हम दोनो मे पर

बड़ी ही बेरुखी से मुँह मोड कर छोड़ दिया हाथ हमारा
फासलों को बता कर ज़िम्मेदार तोड़ दिया दिल हमारा

(3)

क्यों ना एक बार फिरसे तुमको आज़माया जाये
क्यों ना इन फासलों को ज़रा क़रीब किया जाये

मै मजबूर हूँ इन फासलों के आगे पर
मै मज़बूत हूँ इन आँखों के आगे पर

Ujjwal Sharan

"Ujjwal Sharan is undergraduate student of Rajasthan University of Health & Sciences and Co -author of Betiyaan: Udna hai Aaj aur Abhi!" He is a posologist by profession. He is also a conversion optimization writer, specializing in split testing best practices and cognitive biases.

"He has always written blog posts about life lessons, writing his thought was practical. He thought poetry was just for mysterious literary writers. But he was wrong. Secretly, earlier this year, he began to write poetry. Reading and w riting makes him think new ideas dramatically change the way he perceived the old ones. It is a way to process experiences, visual descriptions, and emotions.

(1)

राहे थक जाती है देख-देख कर
निगाहों का क्या करें,
राहे थक जाती है देख-देख कर
निगाहों का क्या करें
सियाही रूक जाती है गिर-गिर कर
इन जज्बातों का क्या करें,
जान बन जाते है लोग जान-जान कर
जान बन जाते है लोग जान-जान कर
इन अपनो का क्या करें,
मरने लगा हु मै जी-जी कर
मरने लगा हु मै जी-जी कर
इस जीने का क्या करें,
और दिल तो आता है उस खतवाले पर रह-रह कर
दिल आता है उस खतवाले पर रह-रह कर
ये तिंदर विंदर् का हम क्या करें।

(2)

अब इततर की बोतलों पर धुल चढी है,
अब इततर की बोतलों पर धुल चढी है।
तेरे जाने के बाद उसका महकना वी भुल चुकी हैं।
किताबें कब से अलमारी में है,
किताबें कब से अलमारी में है।
न जाने गुलाब का क्या हश्र हुआ है,
किताबें है,
गुलाब है और खत भी है
किताबे है,
गुलाब है और खत भी है
पर अलमारी के ताले पे अब धुल चढी है।
उनमें कैद जज्बात पढना वो भुल चुकी है
तेरे जाने के बाद उसका महकना वो भुल चुकी हैं।

Dipshikha Mohanty

"Let your efforts speak of it's wonders"
is the tagline added to her name..
Dipshikha from being a writer has learnt how to write poems and earning up the title of a poet is huge for her. She is a teacher , a social activist and a student too. She writes her mind and mostly scripts on nature, love, life, experiences, etc and even   loves to capture the world through the camera lens. Recently she completed her B. Ed from Nellore and wants to pursue more. She is a dreamer and believes in turning it all into reality.
She is the founder of Dramatic Words and Finesse Talent Hub.

Long Distance Relationship

Meeting over tinder,
Swiping right each other
it was a match,
Neither hello nor hi at first.

Pandemic fell at our foot,
Everyone was locked inside their huts,
boredom was the phase,
that tied us back together with ace.

Eating, sleeping, browsing had become a hobby,
until we connected each other with a 'Hi'.
Chats increased,
Even our destination matched.

It's seemed as if we were meant to be,
Until it striked us that long distance relationship it is,
Nothing mattered to us at all,
As, virtual meeting was the new normal.

Smiling, laughing, dating we went,
As we knew the new normal wouldn't end.
Being away from each other was our fate,
But we were connected by heart.

Someday we would meet for sure we knew,
Let's thing go virtually was the only clue.
That's how we're managing our ship of life and not letting it
sink,
Yes,
Long distance relationship it is.

Love in Distance

I was standing in the balcony
sipping my hot cup of tea
and watching the rain drops kissing the plants and the soil
passionately.
Thinking about how romantic would it be
if you were here with me.
But, unfortunately
This long-distance relationship has spoiled it all for both you
and me.

I know how difficult it is to live without you
Having no clue
of when my dreams would come true
I wish the day comes soon.
I hope our love wouldn't have any boundaries of its own.
This long-distance relationship won't be the barrier in our
bond.

Sneha Dubey

Sneha Dubey is a 12th standard students and seventeen years old. She is a commerce student in Sanskriti Public School from Gorakhpur. She holds a hobby of sketching portraits. She also likes singing songs and acting. In future, she wants to become a chartered accountant.

Long Distance Relationship!!!

Many times, it happens, people don't understand the true value, true meaning of love. But when it comes to a relationship in which distance is long, one understands its true meaning. It seems beautiful and impressive in listening but when you come into it, you understand that it's just like a cage in which two persons are eventually trapped somewhere in the want of something which can be either success or prosperity.

This type of relationship is like two persons have geographic gap between them but their hearts are tied up in beautiful bond of love, souls are conjoined. The distance maintains the bond and the relationship stays strong because two persons feel and realise the need and happiness of staying together. When they do not have a face -to-face contact for days, it increases the craze to have a look at the beloved one. It is basically different from close relation in which you can meet every day or whenever you want.

Now...if we talk about couples!!!then...
Staying away sometimes creates doubt in mind that your partner is cheating you and dating someone else. You must firstly find out the real truth than to blame on your partner with little knowledge of the matter.

If it is possible for you to meet your partner...i would suggest to meet atleast on ce a month, otherwise a negative feeling starts to generate   that distance is between hearts not cities.

The spice adder social media   sites. Instagram , fb, whatsapp etc...creates more doubt if one is active and talking to someone...the other one starts to ignore his|her partner. It creates a silence zone and silence increases emotional gap. So

never let a communication gap come between you and your partner.

Some of you think that gap must be there in relationship!! if i am not wrong!!
Well, it should be there but in limit else it can kill the whole relation.

Have some patience and let your relation stay strong and healthy. Loyalty is the only thing that matters here not the distance.

Rajesh Satpate

नमस्कार प्यारे दोस्तों,

मेरा नाम राजेश सतपते है। मै उप्पूगुडा, शिवाजी नगर हैदराबाद का निवासी हूं। वर्तमान में मै पीजीडीबीएम की पढ़ाई उस्मानिया विश्वविद्यालय से कर रहा हूं।मैंने एम.टेक,बीएससी, बी.टेक, किया है। मेरे परिवार में मेरे पापा और माताजी (श्री रामदास और श्रीमती कलवाती बाई सतपते का व्यवसाय चप्पल रिपेयरिंग का हैं) और मेरी छोटी प्यारी सी बहन हैं जिसका नाम सतपते सुनीता (बी ए - की पढ़ाई डॉ.बी आर अम्बेडकर सार्वत्रिक विश्वविद्यालय से की है। वर्तमान में एम बी ए की पढ़ाई करने जा रही हैं।)मैंने लेखन प्रतियोगिता 8 वर्ष की उम्र से किया है, बाल कविताएं, निबंध लेखन, कहानियां विद्यालय और विश्व विद्यलय में पढ़ते हुए " दैनिक हिन्दी मिलाप वार्ता पत्रिका" के माध्यम से की है।मुझे अभी तक लेख , कहानी, व्यंग और कविता लेखन प्रतियोगिता में " दैनिक हिन्दी मिलाप वार्ता पत्रिका" की ओर से राष्ट्रीय स्तर पर पुरस्कार जानी मानी राज्य सरकार की राजनैतिक हस्तियों द्वारा प्रदान किया गया है।

संपर्क सूत्र :

Instagram I'd: rajesh.Satpate

E-mail: smsrks18@gmail.com

विषय: लंबे वक्त के रिश्ते

यह रिश्ते अपने और अजीब होते हैं,

रिश्ते कुछ खास होते हैं,

ईश्वर से बनकर आते हैं यह रिश्ते,

एक जीवन, अनेक रिश्ते,

जीवन से जुड़े सारे रिश्ते,

फर्क होता है रिश्तो में और रिश्ते में,

जन्म और मरण के बीच में हजारों रिश्ते बन जाते हैं,

किसी से दर्द का रिश्ता होता है,

किसी से प्यार का रिश्ता होता है,

निभें तो सात जन्मों का,

बड़े लंबे समय तक,

कई रंग में रंगे दिखते हैं ,

यह रिश्ते रिश्वत जैसे है

कभी अजनबी अपना बन जाता है,

और अपना अजनबी बन जाता है

रिश्तों से ही आदमी बने गरीब-अमीर,

यह रिश्ते जिंदगी को संवार ते हैं वह बिखर भी देते हैं, हमारा सबसे

अच्छा रिश्ता तो खुदा से होता है जो,

ये रिश्ता सबसे लंबा और लंबे समय तक चलने वाला, क्योंकि यह

रिश्ता खुद, खुदा की मर्जी से बनता है,

क्योंकि वह चाहे तो पल में रिश्ता,

बनता भी है और बिगड़ता भी है,

हर एक रिश्ता नाम के साथ जुड़ा है,

संबंध के साथ जुड़ा होता है,

यह रिश्ते बड़ी अजीब चीज है,

मानव को मानव का मोह होता है,

और वह मोह में इतना आगे निकलता है,

सच क्या है गलत क्या है और क्या करना चाहिए, कितने लंबे समय
तक का रिश्ता,
उसमें एक गहराई होती है ,
विश्वास होता है और,
अपनापन होता है,
जो हर किसी के साथ नहीं होता,
,जो दिल से लगाव होता है,
वह उस व्यक्ति के साथ अपने को दिखने लगता है, सपने देखता है,
उसे अपना मानता है और छोटी सी भी छोटी बात, उसके साथ शेर
की जाती है लेकिन,
लेकिन कहां है ना वक्त किसी का नहीं होता,
समय किसी का नहीं होता,
वक्त और रिश्ते दोनों का ऐसा होता है,
पल में रिश्ते बन जाते हैं वह पल में टूट भी जाते हैं,
वह तो अपने आप चलता है,
ना किसी के लिए रुकता है इसीलिए तो लोग कहते हैं, समय
बलवान हो तो सब अच्छा वरना सब बुरा है,
स्वार्थ से जुड़े रिश्ते मतलब से जुड़े रिश्ते,
उसमें अपनापन नहीं होता,
जब तक आप खुद का मतलब निकलता है,
तब तक वह चलता है सफलता है,
जिस दिन वो रिश्ते में रुकावट आई,
वह रिश्ता भी बेजा़नसा बन जाता है
बरसों से चला आता रिश्ता,
जिसमें हम जीते हैं मरते हैं,
ऊसके अलावा कुछ नहीं होता,
समय समय का मान है,
समय समय की जरूरत है,
समय सबसे बड़ा है,
हम खुद बिखर जाते हैं टूट जाते हैं,

जैसे हमारा कुछ नहीं बचा और हम मन ही मन से, अपने आपको
ही भला बुरा बोलते हैं यह क्या, किया इतना पूरी जिंदगी इस रिश्ते
में लगा दी,
फिर भी यह अपना नहीं होता,
सच्चा, विश्वास दिल से बना रिश्ता,
हम अगर अलग हो जाते हैं,
तो भी वह रिश्ता अपना ही रहेगा ,
क्योंकि दिल से जुड़े रिश्ते कभी नहीं टूटता,
चाहे हम पास हो चाहे दूर हो,
फिर भी यह रिश्ते, खास होते हैं,
क्योंकि दिल से जोड़े रिश्ते कभी खत्म नहीं होते
अंत तक चलते है,
उसका वजूद होता है,
लंबे वक्त के रिश्ते अलग हो जाते हैं बिछड़ जाते हैं,
फिर भी साथ बीते लम्हों को याद करके जीते हैं,
शायद एक दूसरे के जज़्बात को समझते हैं वह अपने आपको
महसूस करते हैं,
इसलिए रिश्ता वही सही,
जो दूर है कि पास है और उसमें कोई,
गलतफहमी नहीं होती उसको महसूस किया जाता है, और जहां पर
हम रहते हैं,
लंबे वक्त के रिश्ते तो उसके,
जरूरी नहीं हमेशा साथ रहो पास रहो कोई आस, रखो, फिर भी
जीवित रहते हैं,
जिस ईश्वर ने हम को बनाया,
उसके साथ हमारा सबसे लंबा रिश्ता है,
कभी हमने ईश्वर को देखा?
कोई भी रूप में कोई भी हालत में,
आकर हमारी मदद करके,
वह चला जाता है फिर भी,

हम बिन देखे उसके ऊपर भरोसा करते हैं
उसकी प्रार्थना करते हैं उसी से मन्नतें मांगते हैं,
इसी तरह जो रिश्ता हमने बनाया है ,
उसकी आंखें बंद कर कर हमें भरोसा होना चाहिए, उसमें विश्वास
होना चाहिए ,
और वह अपना होना चाहिए ,
जीतना ज्यादा समय उसके साथ,
उससे प्रेम लगन सब कुछ आता है,
समय के साथ उसकी,
अलग हो जाते हैं लेकिन कभी हो अपने आपको या सामने वाले
व्यक्ति को नुकसान नहीं पहुंचाता,
अपने और उसकी रिश्ते की कदर करते हैं,
मेरे मतलब से तो,
बिन स्वार्थ का रिश्ता ही सच्चा रिश्ता होता है और लंबे वक्त से मैं तो
यह होना बहुत जरूरी है,
शायद उनकी डोर उस प्रभु के पास होती है।

Nuzair Fathima

A young mother who is an aspiring writer and poetess   . An aspiring writer, a poetess, a philographer with passion to pen down reality and emotions.

Long Distance Relationship

Our relationship stands strong,
But the distance very long.
Sitting in our room and wondering,
What in that country might you be doing?
Miles apart, but always in my heart,
Love still sweet like a tart.
Physically you may be absent,
But in my mind, you are present.
9 years of special bonding,
A bond that's never ending.
Come what problem, or calamity,
You remain my first priority.
Yearning for your hug, yearning for your touch,
I keep reminding I miss you so much.
Looking at the smaller version of you,
I smile imagining him with you.
Friends and family I do have around,
But I keep searching for your sound.
When you are with me, I feel complete,
Without you life seems like a plain sheet.
Cherishing our everlasting memories,
I pen them down in summaries.

(2)

Waiting for the days for the distance to end,
Waiting For my love and my best friend.
Our moments together I do cherish,
For never will they ever perish.
A gush of wind on my face blew,
A smile on my lips with a thought of you.
Admiring our little son,Who's having lot of fun,
I know you love him and miss him tons.
The time runs fast when we are together,
It runs slow when we're away from each other.
Throughout the day your thoughts on mind,
Throughout the night our memories rewind.
I pen my feelings which were left untold,
New chapters of life we will unfold.
With you by my side I want to grow,
Living today imagining tomorrow.
I love you to my heart's core,
I miss you every day little more.

Shivi Goyal

Author who travels is what she is known for. Awardee of two prestigious book awards. She is solo traveling since there were no drone and go pro. Her books and blogs focus on positivity of life and traveling to unknown places. She expresses her gratitude and feelings with her artwork in the name of Mystopedia Creations.

If Your Love of Life Is Far Apart, This One Is for You…

I yearn for you
Can't breathe without you
I'm counting days
The meaningless life is killing
Life seems miserable until we meet again
Missing you is not just the TERM
It is, every single second stitched in 1000 miles
Waiting for the highways to crunch into them
Roads shall become familiar with her presence
I wish I could unravel her presence close to me
I wish I could freeze her tears
Making her eyes even more beautiful
She isn't here to comfort me
However, when I awake it seems real
Believe, that you will be near to me soon.

My Sunshine

Hey darling, this is what you are for me
Hey Love, you are my sunshine
Bringing light to my dark world
Putting sweet memories in longings
You are the shining armor to my lingering loneliness
You bring stillness to my wheezing heart
She is delightfully chaotic when she Is into her silk robe
She is a beautiful mess when in her frizzy hair
She is seductive in her smile
That smile has something to yearn for
Enough to believe in
Enough to believe for
Enough to fight for
And then….
Her soft arms embrace all of my dusks
Just like my nightfall got filled with twilight shine
To beckon my dreamland
To put my paraphernalia into silent mode
It's when I think of her more strong
Closer, in me, all of me…
Hey my sunshine, your light, kindled up my world
Miles apart, not for a second, I feel
You aren't with me
Rather, you are the enlightenment into my sunset
Waving a kiss on a forehead
Hey, sunshine, come soon, coz, I love you.

Prachi Sharna

Her name is Prachi Sharma, and is currently residing in Ghaziabad, a district in U.P. She is pursuing BSc Maths from Ccs University.

She has participated in more than 30 anthologies so far. She wrote a book 'Feelingin Words' which is available on Google Play Books. Also, she has compiled three anthologies: "Write to Feel Not to Explain," "Writer's World" "First Day" And Ansune Khayal .She has participated in few Record anthologies. "KAVYANJALI" was founded by her which is an online Instagram platform that provides various opportunities to writers and helps them to develop their skills. Give your feedback on her E-mail: - prachisharma51689@gmail.com or you can contact her on Instagram Id: - (@sharma0162)

<u>कहाँ है वो पागल सी लड़की?</u>

बहुत देर होगी है
ना कोई मैसेज
ना कोई कोल
ना कोई वो स्टीकर वाला खेल

कहाँ है वो आज पागल सी लड़की
क्या कोई लड़ाई हुई है
या क्या कोई आज अपना रूठा है तुमसे
क्या कोई गिला है या कोई शिकवा

कोई रूठा है तो मना लो
कोई गुस्सा है तो उसका गुस्सा खत्म करो
कोई लड़ाई है तो बंद करो
मिता दो सारे गिले शिकवे तुम्हारे

अब ये चुप्पी मुझे भी बहुत चुभ रही है
जो हुआ सुलझा लो ना
फिर से शुरू करो वही तुम्हारा सिलसिला
जो मुझे तुमसे ज्यादा प्यारा है

Career

Career is nothing to you all,
But it's my upcoming identity
It is my identity which needs nothing but me, my effort and my complete determination.
It is that identity which does not require any kind of relationship.
I will be known just because of my courage, my determination and my effort.
Yes, I am completely crazy to achieve my own identity.
Yes, I am mad fully to know from me not because of anyone else.
I love my career and passionate for it,
Because it takes a long time to come to me but always stay with me.
What can I achieve by myself? Never destroy
My ambition, my goal never leaves me alone, never cheat me
They hurt me firstly but give me life time happiness.
And I love this happiness

Yashvi Yashi Srivastava

A student from Gorakhpur city. Who has a great interest in reading, debating and writi ng. She likes to put a lot of her emotions, experiences, and opinions into what she writes and loves being able to make her writing something that other people can connect to, or relate to in some way by generalizing the thoughts and experiences she's writing about.
And she did her debut in the writing field from Aaryansh Arora's anthology Happy in Us.

Long Distance Relationship-
Separation of Bodies Not Their Souls

The very moment someone says those three words our mind runs to a conclusion that says 'Long distance relationship is something that is very painful separation and is experienced by two people who are in a relationship' right?Now according to me it also means that firstly relationship can be of any type ...relation of a father and son ; mother and daughter; sister and brother . And living apart from any of them gives a lot of pain but then there are situations which leads to such separations it can be your   work, studies or anything!But we should also think in this way that how can working or studying for a better future that would give you and your loved one a life full of happiness be painful? Sometimes a temporary happiness leads us to a

permanent guilt . So think in a better way . Whether separation is between you and your wife , girlfriend, parents , siblings or anyone keep this one thing in your mind that distance is between two bodies living at different places not between their souls....your souls are connected ...your roots are always connected.So at last all that matters is that you should focus on your present work & task that has separated you from your loved one . Give your 100% then meet them with a sense of positivity and achievement that the pain which all of you experienced and hard work which you did ignoring the pain of living apart didn't go waste. Make that separation a cause of your success. It will make that long distance worthy.

Ayushi Sharma

I'm Ayushi Sharma from Gwalior district of MP. I'm currently studying BSc Mathematics from Jiwaji University. I love sketching. And I also like to write stories. I want to become a professional sketching artist.

मेरी सबसे अच्छी दोस्तः रिया

दोस्ती एक साथ जो हमेशा हर मुश्किल मे हमारे साथ रहते हैं | चाहे कितनी भी मुश्किल कयूं ना आजाए हमारी लाइफ में वो हर मुश्किल से निकलने में मदद करते हैं | एसी ही कुछ हमारी भी दोस्ती है | मेरे स्कूल बदलने के बाद पता नहीं था | मैं तुझसे मिलूंगी और हमारी दोस्ती इतनी खास हो जाएगी, कि बोलने से पहले ही हम एक दूसरे की बातें समझ जाया करेंगे | पहले तो मैं तुझसे बात तक नहीं किया करती थीं लोगों की बातों में आकर तुझे बुरी समझा करती थीं पर मैं गलत थी एक तू ही थी और हैं जो हमेशा मेरे लिए लड़ा करती हैं | जब लोगों ने मुझे गलत समझा जब उनने मुझसे बात करना बंद कर दिया मुझे बहुत बुरा बोला तब बस तू ही थी जो हमेशा मेरे साथ खड़ी रहती थी | जब तूने मेरे लिए दूसरो से बात करना बंद किया था तब पता चला था दोस्त सिर्फ दोस्त कहने से नहीं होते | दोस्ती का मतलब भी पता होना चाहिए और तुझसे अच्छी बेस्ट फ्रेंड मुझे कभी नहीं मिल ही नहीं सकती | जब तूने मुझे पहली बार बोला था मुझे बेस्ट फ्रेंड बनाना पसंद नहीं क्यूंकि कोई बेस्ट फ्रेंड का मतलब ही नहीं जानता है पर तूने मेरे साथ समय बिताया और मुझे समझा और जब तूने एक दिन मुझे बेस्ट फ्रेंड बोला मैं बता नहीं सकती मुझे कितना स्पेशल फील हुआ था | लोग कहते थे कि तू फ्रेंडशिप निभाने के लायक नहीं हैं पर तूने उस दोस्ती को बहुत अच्छे से निभाया है और आज भी निभाती हैं और मुझे समझती है रिया बस यही कहना चाहूंगी तू हमेशा मेरे साथ रहना मुझे कभी छोड़कर मत जाना क्यूंकि तेरी मेरी यारी सबसे प्यारी हैं | बस सबसे यही कहूँगी उनको दोस्त बनाओ जो दोस्ती का मतलब जानते है जो हर मुश्किल में साथ रहते हैं | उनको नहीं जो दोस्ती को सिर्फ मजाक समझते हैं जो मतलब वाली दोस्ती करते हैं आज काम हैं तो बात कर लिया वरना कभी हाल भी नहीं पूछते |

Nilesh Vispute he is a mechanical engineer by profession. He love to write shayri, poem, micro tale specially he write on love and motivation.

The 10 Minute Taxi Trip

On my way to home after the hectic semester exam I was tired to the extent if someone tries to kidnap me I may not resist. Hopping from one song to another finding a perfect song to listen that dwell with my present situation I took a taxi on my way to home. I was so tired, clumsy & agitated that it took me a minute to settle into the taxi while gathering myself up My eyes went to a girl sitting opposite to me in the taxi .approx same age as of mine She was wearing a lab coat (probably a medical student I guess) over a salwar suit seems like dress code of any college with a student bag may be for carrying books presumably I wish I could define how she looks but she was wearing a pale safron piece of cloth all along the length of shoulder covering the whole face leaving only eyes unsleeved I unravel the first plot twist those eyes were the only one which seems so familiar like nothing else giving me a vibe just as if I have known those eyes for emulsifying decades I can still feel the vibe of those while That too were fatigued by the frenetic day .I was in a dilemma of asking how to ask her If we know each other tosome expanse ?? suddenly I noticed her feets were humming to any beat but she didn't wore any kind of hearing aids .She was throbbing in a periodic manner also sometimes a hard to notice swinging of head in between I wish I could have fondle the vibe she w as giving but my timidity again won our destination were common suddenly an old lady came along presumably for riding along when she was trying to enter into the taxi she accidentally slipped, Even before I could come 0 forward to help her the girl who was opposite to me helped her and pull her up bare handedly I don't know why I was fallen for her matured behavior and evasive execution also knowing the fact that this thing will last for another stop and we will both charge forward to our own particular destination in life still mind was fighting a undisclosed war

with himself a dilemma on wheather to ask who is she is but I also wasn't able to resist the pleasure gazing her temptress eyes wishing God to extend the commute a little more stretch the span a little more slugg the time a little more.

Flairs and Glairs, a platform by a student for the students. We are esteemed youth struggling to carve out our path for our future and we follow a basic mindset Since everyone is not born with allround skills. Joining hands with people who are born to execute it with perfection is the best way to evol ve. Self-Evolution is the need of the hour but, evolving as a community is what we strive for. The initiative as kickstarted by, Founder - Mr. Shubham Shah with the motive to utilize the skillset and talent of writing has now a team of 10+ people who are actively participating into newer forms of learning and discovering talents among youngsters. We Provide platform and services like Publishing opportunities, Open mics, Workshops, Hands-on training. Operating with Brand Name of Flairs and Glairs (Publication House), we offer the chance of elevating a passionate writer to an esteemed author   With Brand name Teekhe Zasbaaat. We bring to you an opportunity to get accustomed with the Public Speaking and Presenting of Thoughts along with regular challen ges to brush up your inking spirit.   The newest initiative to extend our services we introduced in a new writing Platform- The Glittering Fables and Ink Over Tears.

We Choose to Fly Like A Falcon than to be

a Leg Pulling Crab.

To Know More: Infoline – 7781900870
Mail Us At-
flairsandglairs@gmail.com / info@flairsandglairs.in
Or Visit is at
www.flairsandglairs.com / www.flairsandglairs.in
Social Handles- @flairsandglairs @teekhezasbaaat